lazy, crazy & amaZing

story by S F Hochman

The ZequIllustration

illustrations by: *Kaylynn Leaper, Joseph Luciano, Julianne Belardo, Kelly Chin,*
Maddie McMonagle, Ben Graham/Matt Strickland, Samantha Stout, Kyle Smith, Carley Polan,
Andreina Garcia-Gomez, Carli Mendelow, Paige Shaw, Angelica Rivera, Colleen McGill, Tyler Krasnigor

D1367080

Contest and *ZequIllustration*...

As soon as I finished writing laZy, craZy & amaZing, I took it to several educational venues to read to a range of age groups. Children, teachers and adult reader volunteers encouraged me to publish this book immediately. Who am I to argue with such a fervent public outcry? I put the book in front of the most fastidious readers I knew to proof it and then self-published.

I took the published but visually unadorned book to more schools. While the kids' imaginations virtually painted every scene in their minds, most still wanted to see pictures. In fact, many of them started sketching Z and Dr. Letterberger. In our discussions after the readings, more than a few expressed their desire to illustrate the story. After more than thirty years of professional writing, at the precipice of publishing my first book, I found myself contemplating the possibility of putting my work's fate in the petite and untrained hands of children. What a craZy idea!

As if mirroring the theme of this story, craZy evolved into amaZing! My wife suggested, "have an illustration contest!" Brilliant! (As usual, thank you, dear.) With help from Rhonda Shevrin, Director of BookMates of South Jersey (a great organization), and other school contacts, I set off on a "craZy and amaZing book and Illustration Contest" tour. I didn't keep an exact count, but I'm sure I had the privilege of sharing laZy, craZy & amaZing with more than 2,000 eager listeners and potential illustrators. (Full disclosure: *not* all were that eager to illustrate.) I received a few hundred submissions from students in first to fifth grade. You'll find the winning illustrations lighting up almost every page of this book. Though the story hasn't changed, the renderings give it more color and depth. Being different, but still the same, I couldn't accurately call it a sequel. In fact, I couldn't find any word to appropriately define it. So, I've made one up. This is the first known (at least to me) *ZequIllustration!*

I hope you enjoy the young artists' mini-masterpieces as much as I do. FYI, the contest was freeform, allowing artists to draw any scene their minds imagined. Consequently, you'll see Dr. Letterberger as a young woman with dark hair in some illustrations. Somewhat older with light hair in others. And, as a kind of hybrid being, more beef and bun than flesh and blood. Responding to this creative interpretation, I thought it best to change the spelling of the good doctor's name to "Letter**burger**."

I hope this *burger* talk has given you an appetite to read on and that the story and illustrations give you plenty of *food for thought.*

Hoc

Please read more about the contest, the winners and the overall experience of writing and delivering this story at the end of the book. If you have the time, let me know what you think about Z's journey and the idea of having kids illustrate the story. You can email me at: hoc@doandyouwilllearn.com I'll be glad to post constructive comments — and praise — for the story and illustrations on the Z pages of www.doandyouwilllearn.com.

To Marci, Cooper, Dylan, Joey, Josh, Matt and, of course, Alissa, AKA Dr. Letterburger... and in memory of Charlie, the beloved grandkitty I never got to read with

laZy, craZy & amaZing

It was past six o'clock and Dr. Letterburger was getting tired. She had heard enough problems for one day, but she had taken an oath to serve others and heal their fragile minds. She buzzed her receptionist to see if she had more patients.

"Just one," came the reply.

"Okay, send him in."

"Be careful," whispered the receptionist. "This one has been in the waiting room all day and –"

Before the receptionist could finish her sentence, the doctor's door swung open. But she saw no one. She looked to the left.

She looked to the right. At last, she looked down and spied a very stressed out little character. Her natural instinct was to meet anger with more anger, but at the University of MAMA (the school of Mind Adjustment and Mending Attitudes) Dr. Letterburger had learned to defuse *situations* with calm and friendliness.

"Hello there. So nice to meet you. I'm Dr. Alissa Letterburger."

The character seemed to look up at her, but she wasn't sure.

His face, if it was a face, was kind of hard to read. When he didn't say anything, she asked. "Would you kindly tell me who you are?…"

"What? You don't recognize me?" said the little guy in a zizzy-zany voice.

The doctor shrugged.

"All those fancy diplomas on your wall and you don't know who I am?"

"If I had to guess, I'd say you kind of look like the letter Z."

"Zippity-do-dah, the doctor knows her alphabet."

"No need to get zippy. I've had a not so good day and you're my last patient. And –"

"Of course, I'm last. I'm always last!" complained the 26th letter. "It doesn't matter when I'm ready. Everyone always goes before me."

Julianne Belardo, Grade 4, Larchmont Elementary

"Well, we have an order here. And, it's alphabetical," said the doctor as calmly as possible.

"A to Z. Always A to Z. Never Z to A," lamented little Z.

"So, Z, what brings you here today?" The doctor spoke while she started a new file labeled "Z," two files behind her X file.

"I'm tired," said Z.

The doctor responded reflexively. "Do you exercise?"

"Do I look out of shape?" Z shot back.

Dr. Letterburger was trained to observe the mind not the body, but as far as she could tell he looked in pretty good shape, for a Z. She normally would follow up by asking about eating and sleeping habits, but the doctor decided to be more direct and ask, "are you sad or depressed?"

Kelly Chin, Grade 3, Carson Elementary, Pennsauken

"Wouldn't you be if you were last all the time?… I'm not tired, tired. I'm TIRED OF BEING LAST!"

"I see," she said. Other than empathizing, there really wasn't much the doctor could do. The little guy was a Z. Being last was the destiny of all Zees. She never even gave thought to the idea that being last would bother a Z. She decided to shake his family tree a bit.

"I'm assuming your father is a Z?"

"Yes."

"And your mother? – "

"A *Zee*."

"How do they handle being last?"

"My father is laZy. He'd probably be last even if he was a G or an H."

The doctor scribbled down a note in the Z file: ***lazy father.***

"And my mother is craZy. She has a biZarre outlook. She thinks last is good."

The doctor added resents mother to his file, then asked about other family members.

"My sister Zigs. My brother Zags. My uncle is totally Zoned out. My grandparents are either in a daZe or a haZe. And just last week my aunt got Zapped."

The doctor jotted down another note: subject has **no family role models.** She went to the next area of concern. "How's your work going?"

"Not great. I don't get used nearly as much as most letters and when I do it's usually not in a good way."

"What do you mean not in a good way?"

The letter handed the doctor his work schedule from the previous week: He was used fifteen times by third graders who made fun of a little boy for messing up on a test. ***"Bobby got a Zero, Zero, Zero, Zero…You're a Zero! Zero! Zero!"***

Ben Graham/Matt Strickland, Grade 5, Moorestown U.E.

A national newspaper pasted him into a very unflattering headline that read, "Angry Zealots Burn Books!" And, dozens of parents called on him when they needed to yell at their teenagers for "sitting on the couch all day and doing Zilch!"

"Zilch!" Z cried. "I hate being part of that word. It's so harsh!"

The doctor wanted to tell the little letter that her very own daughter's favorite place was the ZOO. Then she remembered how the little darling nagged over and over again to take her to the zoo.

Samantha Stout, Grade 5, Springfield Elementary

"Take me to the ZOO. You promised to take me to the ZOO. Zoo… zoo… Take me. Take me... zoo… zoo… Mommy zoo… zoo... Mommy, mommy take me ZOO ZOO ZOO!" As much as she wanted to, Dr. Letterburger could not utter the word "zoo" out loud in a positive light. She opened another file marked "Me" and scribbled down: *seek therapy.*

Dr. Letterburger took a couple of deep breaths then mustered up enough courage to ask the big question.

"So, what would you like to happen?"

"I would like to move up in the alphabet."

"I'm sorry, I'm afraid Z will always come after a-b-c-d-e-f-g and all the rest."

"Then maybe I don't want to be a Z anymore," the proud letter said holding back a tear or two.

Dr. Letterburger felt the little letter's pain. She wanted to go over to the couch and give him a hug, but she didn't know where. He was all edges and end points. Not very cuddly. In fact, not cuddly at all. Then she had an idea. It would take a little effort and some re-adjusting on his part.

"You know Z, now that I'm looking at you, I think if we just turned you on your side and you went on a little diet, you could pass for an N."

Wow, an N, thought Z. "Then I wouldn't be last anymore, would I?"

"Heck, no. You'd be 14 out of 26. Pretty much in the middle," the doctor said with a twinkle of hope.

"N," pondered Z. "N is for no, not, nuclear weapons, never, nasty, naughty and nothing. Nobody will like me if I'm nasty or naughty. And, being nothing that's EVEN WORSE THAN ZERO!" Z sounded more agitated.

Dr. Letterburger took another look at Z and started sketching something into his file. "You know, there's a surgeon down the hall who may be able to remove one of your lines. Then you could look kind of like this <."

Z looked at the doctor's drawing. "What's that? Two crooked lines? I'd look like a back arrow or a bracket that software geeks use. I'm not a symbol. I'm a letter!"

"Okay, okay," said the doctor, riding the wave of another idea. "After we remove one line, with a little physical therapy, you could learn to stand on your point. Then you could be a **V!**"

"V?" Z thought about it for a second. "That's not much further up the alphabet."

"It's used in some very positive ways. V for VICTORY," said Doc Letterburger cheerfully. "V for inVincible."

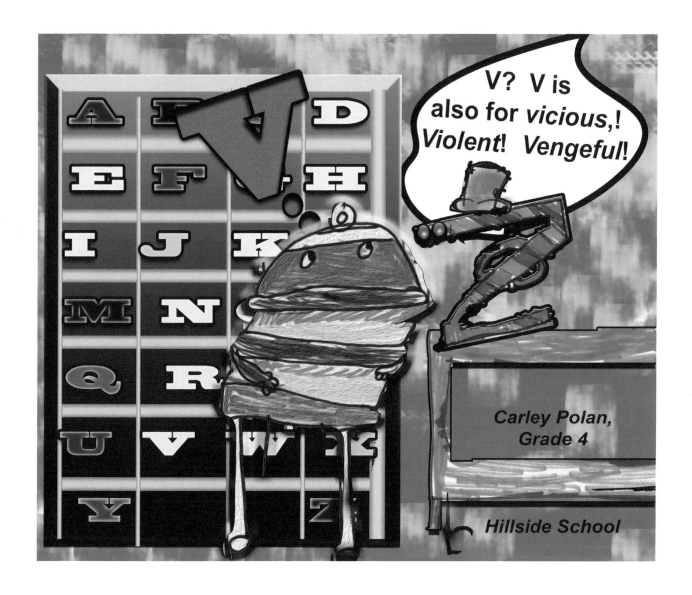

"V is also for vicious, violent, vengeful, eVicted," the Z countered. "Surgery then therapy to become a V? Seems like a lot of work just to wind up a mean, one-angle letter."

The doctor saw Z's point, but she also saw the clock approaching seven. She threw out a new, less drastic idea. "How flexible are you?"

"Why?"

"Yes, Y," the doctor said, sketching out a blueprint for how Z could be stretched and twisted into the 25th letter.

Andreina Garcia-Gomez,
Grade 3, Whittier School

"Are you kidding?" Z asked. "I could never be a Y. Why would anyone want to be a Y? They're one place ahead of us in the alphabet and they think they're better than us. But in real life, we're always ahead of them. Crazy, lazy, hazy, cozy, oozy. Then they start whining about why they have to follow Z. If I became a Y, my family would X me out."

"X!" exclaimed the doctor. "All we'd have to do is remove your torso, turn your top and bottom 45 degrees and you could be a small X."

"No way!" retorted Z. "I could never be an X. Exes? No one ever says anything nice about their eXes. Do you know what eXes do? They mark questions on tests wrong. Then some poor little kid has to go home and explain all those eXes to his mom or dad or grandmother. No way, doc. I'll never snitch on a kid. I'm not that kind of letter."

"Bet you'd like to be an A," the doctor said, playing into the last letter's ego.

Paige Shaw, Grade 2 Parkway School

"Maybe," Z tried to play it cool. But it was every Zee's dream to become an A. A for All-American. Double A. AAA. A-list. A1. A has such an overblown reputation it's able to replace whole words it doesn't even figure into like A for *Excellent*.

Reading the envy in Z's mind, the doctor decided to break a rule and tell him about another patient. "You know I had an A in here once," the doctor said softly.

"An A here?" Z could not imagine why an A would need to see a head doctor. "What could bother an A? Too loved and too popular?" Z asked snidely. "Yes. She couldn't handle the pressure to always be best. To always be in the forefront. Under the spotlight. She just couldn't lead anymore."

"So what happened?"

"She cracked." The doctor sketched something down and showed it to Z. "Like this."

Z looked at the image of several lines going in different directions. He could hardly tell it was ever a letter, never mind an A. Z winced.

"We took her down to Dr. Pretzelman's office to piece her into something she could handle," Doctor Letterburger said as she drew how the old A now appeared.

"She's a 4?" Z was shocked. "They converted an A into a number."

"And since there was a piece left over, they made her into -4."

Z nearly flat-lined. "She went from being the most envied letter to a negative number?"

There are only 26 letters, an elite, select group. While numbers were in the millions. Billions. Trillions. Gazillions! 4 isn't even a prime number. Suddenly, Z's problems seemed very small. Very small indeed.

"I think Dr. Pretzelman is still in the building," offered Dr. Letterburger knowingly. "What should I tell him YOU would like to become?"

Z took a deep breath. He thought of the A who cracked. He thought of X who was so often wrong. E who got dragged onto the end of words all the time for no real reason. He always admired K for being at the front of noble, edgy and smart words like "knight" and "knife" and "knowledge." Then Z realized that even though he got into important words, K had to stay silent most of the time. Z could never do that.

"I have a voice," Z blurted out proudly.

"A very nice and unique voice," agreed the doctor. "Without you a lot of words would lose their meaning and personality. What would Zoom be without you?"

"Oom?" guessed Z.

"That doesn't sound very fast. Does it?" asked the doctor.

"No."

"Who could take your place in Zebra?… Certainly not A," assured the doctor. "B would make the poor beast a – "

"Bebra?" guessed Z.

"C wouldn't really work unless the animal moved into the water," said the doc trying out more letters in front of the word. "And D would turn a Zebra into a – "

Colleen McGill, Grade 3, Beeler Elementary

"Deebra!" guessed Z.

"*Debra,*" the doctor corrected Z.

"Half the Zebras I know wouldn't like that."

"Probably not," agreed Dr. Letterburger.

Z and Dr. Letterburger agreed that Z's job in the alphabet was pretty important after all. "Okay then. If I'm so important, why must I always come at the very end?" Z cleverly asked the doc.

"You know, we people have a saying. *We save the best for last.*"

"THE best?" asked Z.

"How 'bout if I say *Zee* best?" asked the doctor.

"Oh, I would like that very much," said Z, beginning to glow with pride.

Doctor Letterburger saw a whole new energy come over the letter. "How do you feel now?"

"Zesty!" said Z.

"Good," cheered the doctor getting caught up in the mood change. "You know what?"

"What?"

"Starting tomorrow, every other day, I'm going to take my patients in reverse alphabetical order."

"Z to A instead of A to Z?"

"That's right."

The little Z's self esteem reached a new zenith! Without thinking, he jumped up onto the doctor's desk and planted a big wet kiss on her cheek.

Tyler Krasnigor, Grade 5 Moorestown UE

Z Zoomed home telling everyone along the way that he was proud to be a Z. And, that he, Z, was right in the middle of everything amaZing.

– zee end –

More About the amaZing Illustration Contest...

There were no guidelines for illustrators other than "draw what you imagine when you hear or read the story." Judging was based on relevant content, creativity and quality of the work — in that order. With entries coming from first to fifth graders, judges applied different expectations based on age. As the author and image editor, I was most impressed by subtleties in the pictures and how they advanced or supported the words on the page.

I tweaked, stylized, or edited all illustrations to enhance the story's message or to maintain an artistic consistency throughout the book. I'm very appreciative to the hundreds of budding artists who submitted a creative drawing. Thanks, also, to the teachers, reading specialists and principals who followed through and sent their work to me.

I give *very special thanks* to the illustrators named below. Their work caught my imagination and enriched my story. Keep on drawing!

Kaylynn Leaper, Grade 4, Fleetwood Elementary, Mt. Laurel

Joeseph Luciano, Grade 5, Whittier Elementary, Camden

Julianne Belardo, Grade 4, Larchmont Elementary, Mt. Laurel

Kelly Chin, Grade 3, Carson Elementary, Pennsauken

Maddie McMonagle, Grade 3, Parkway Elementary, Mt. Laurel

Ben Graham/Matt Strickland, Grade 5, Moorestown U.E.

Samantha Stout, Grade 5, Springfield Elementary

Kyle Smith, Grade 4, Fleetwood Elementary, Mt. Laurel

Carley Polan, Grade 4, Hillside Elementary, Mt. Laurel

Andreina Garcia-Gomez, Grade 3, Whittier Elementary, Camden

Carli Mendelow, Grade 2, Bay Village, OH

Paige Shaw, Grade 2, Parkway Elementary, Mt. Laurel

Angelica Rivera, Grade 5, St.Joseph Pro-Cathedral School, Camden

Colleen McGill, Grade 3, Beeler Elementary, Marlton

Tyler Krasnigor, Grade 5, Moorestown U.E.

NOTE TO ADULT READERS...

In 2005, Dorothy and Harold Minkoff *invited* me into the world of BookMates. In my second BookMate season, I found myself in Ms Erin McAnulty's first grade class at Hawthorne Park Elementary School in Willingboro, NJ. I've been *BookMating* there ever since.

What's a BookMate, you ask? The official line reads:

> "BookMates is an interfaith literacy program that provides services to *Title I* elementary schools in low and moderate income communities throughout South Jersey."

While that may not sound like a life-lifting, endorphin releasing activity, believe me it is! In fact, it may be the most invigorating, meaningful and personally rewarding time I have each week!... For a better sense of what the joys and rewards of BookMating or independent volunteer reading are really like, check out the video on the BookMates web page: http://www.jewishsouthjersey.org/page.aspx?id=182174.

Then, get ready to read your heart out. You can start by sharing this story with some of your favorite little people! If you get a chance, let me know how it goes. Email me at: hoc@doandyouwilllearn.com

Thanks again for reading this book and more importantly, thanks for reading to kids. You're making the world a better place... one good read and one child at a time.

SF Hochman

Want the digital and interactive versions of this book and other cool digital stuff?...
Visit www.doandyouwilllearn.com to find out how.

Made in the USA
Charleston, SC
25 May 2013